The books at
PM Animal Facts: Pets
Orange Level

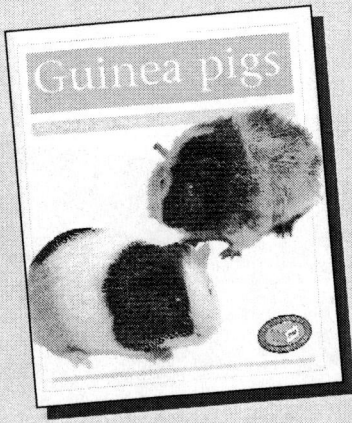

Guinea pigs

Creating the atmosphere

- Encourage the children to talk about pets they know.
- Discuss the differences between animals that are kept as pets and animals in the wild.

Focusing on the book

- Discuss the title and cover page photograph.
- Turn to the title page and talk about the list of contents and the corresponding page numbers.
- Read each chapter heading with the children. Ask them to turn to a chapter of their choice. Check that they are using the page numbers as reference.
- Return to the first chapter on p. 2. Read this with the children, discussing the photographs and/or illustrations.
- Read the linear question of the bottom of the page. Encourage the children to find the answer within the text of this double page. Turn to the next page and confirm the answer which is on the corresponding colour band at the bottom of the page.
- Discuss the reason for the alphabetical index on the inside back cover of the book. Demonstrate how to use the index, then observe and assist the children as they experiment with the new skill.

Going beyond the book

- Make a large poster or drawing of a guinea pig. Make labels of body features on small cards. Have the children take turns to attach the labels to the correct parts of the guinea pig with Velcro© or Blutack©.
- Look at a variety of pictures of animals with different tails. As a class, or in small groups, talk about and compare the size, shape and colour of the tails. Make a chart with the children, showing the different tails.
- Before the children read *Guinea pigs* (PM Animal Facts: Pets) make a facts book or chart listing what they know. Challenge the children to add to the list of facts as they read the book and other related books.
- Write a menu for a pet guinea pig. Ask the children the following questions: What will the guinea pig eat? What will it drink? Have the children write a menu for themselves. Compare the two menus.

> As this is a non-fiction book, each chapter or paragraph can stand alone. Children do not have to hold the thread of a storyline in their minds.

Guinea pig menu

hay
grain
grass
carrots
cabbage leaves
cucumbers
water

My menu

cereal
bread
fruit
vegetables
meat
water
juice
milk

Blackline masters 1 and 2, pp.21–22.

- Have the children make a model of a guinea pig's cage using cardboard. Talk about the importance of including details such as a door.

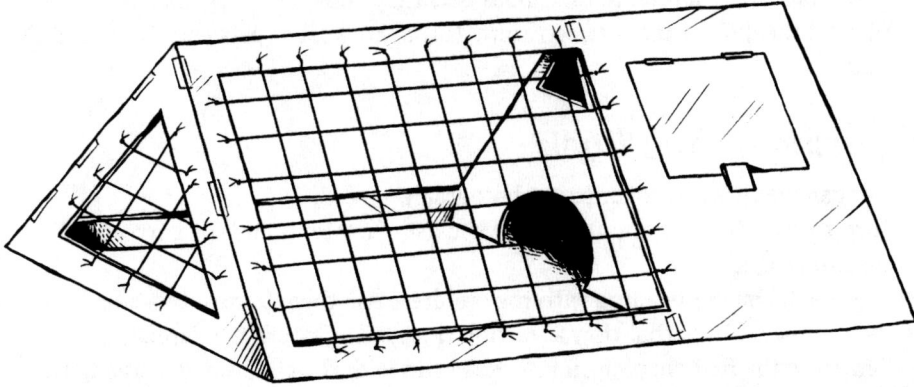

- The children could write their own questions and answers about guinea pigs, from information in the book. They could ask each other their questions.
- Have a real guinea pig or a large poster of a guinea pig available for the children to look at. Ask the children to sketch the guinea pig using pencil.
  Discuss the colours of guinea pigs — refer to p. 2 of *Guinea pigs* (PM Animal Facts: Pets). The children could experiment with colours by mixing paints to achieve tones similar to the colours of the guinea pig. Have them paint their guinea pig sketches and display them on a large cage-shaped mural.

- Make a list of small pets that are kept in cages. Discuss the positive and negative points of having a pet in a confined space.
- Give each child modelling clay to make a model of a guinea pig. They could attach a card to the model with some information about the guinea pig on it.

Reinforce learning in a variety of ways.

Guinea pigs don't have tails.

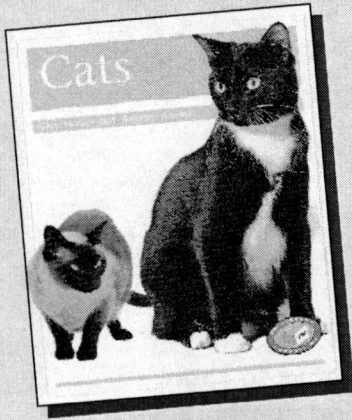

Cats

Creating the atmosphere

- Encourage the children to talk about pets they know.
- Discuss the differences between animals that are kept as pets and animals in the wild.

Focusing on the book

- Discuss the title and cover page photograph.
- Turn to the title page and talk about the list of contents and the corresponding page numbers.
- Read each chapter heading with the children. Ask them to turn to a chapter of their choice. Check that they are using the page numbers as reference.
- Return to the first chapter on p. 2. Read this with the children, discussing the photographs and/or illustrations.
- Read the linear question of the bottom of the page. Encourage the children to find the answer within the text of this double page. Turn to the next page and confirm the answer which is on the corresponding colour band at the bottom of the page.
- Discuss the reason for the alphabetical index on the inside back cover of the book. Demonstrate how to use the index, then observe and assist the children as they experiment with the new skill.

As this is a non-fiction book, each chapter or paragraph can stand alone. Children do not have to hold the thread of a storyline in their minds.

Going beyond the book

- Compare a fiction book such as *Hairy Maclary Scattercat* (Lynley Dodd, Mallinson Rendel, 1988) with the non-fiction book *Cats* (PM Animal Facts: Pets). Discuss the similarities and differences between the two books. Record the children's ideas on a chart.
- View a video about the wild cat family. Discuss similarities and differences between wild cats and domestic cats. Record these facts on a chart.
- Ask the children to use *Cats* (PM Animal Facts: Pets) to find five facts about cats, and to write them down. Encourage the children to make an oral presentation based on these facts to either a small or a large group. Show the children how different visual aids, e.g. posters, pictures, models, and overhead transparencies can enhance their presentations.
- Have a range of non-fiction books about animals available. Make a list of the animals featured in the books. Ask the children to use the books to find out the names of the animals' young, e.g. cats — kittens; dogs — puppies; and cows — calves. Add these words to the list.
- Make a 'knowledge map' with the children, noting everything they know about cats.

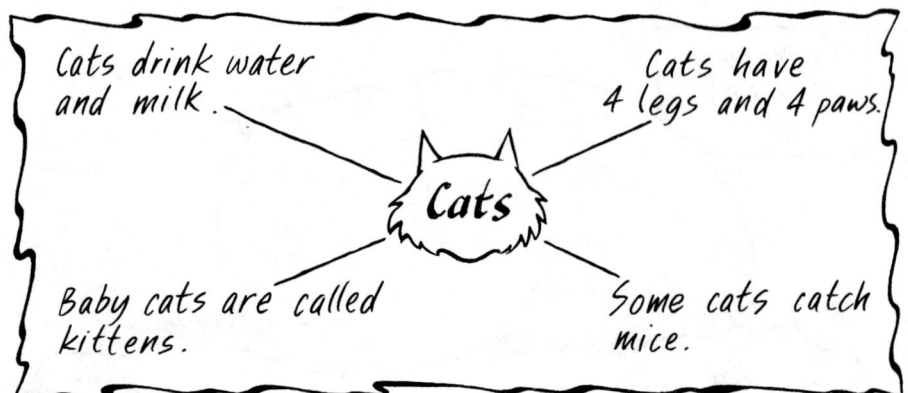

Encourage the children to listen and to interact in small and large group situations.

Ensure that the children know how to search for and extract relevant information from the resources provided.

Cats drink water and milk.

Cats have 4 legs and 4 paws.

Cats

Baby cats are called kittens.

Some cats catch mice.

Blackline masters 3 and 4, pp.23–24.

Cats

- Give the children examples of simple cinquain poems and talk about the purpose of each line. They could then write their own cinquain poem about a cat.

Line 1	The title
Line 2	Describe the title
Line 3	An action
Line 4	A feeling
Line 5	Another title

Cats
Jelly meat eaters
Prowling, pouncing, purring
Cuddly and Soft
Friends to all.

- Go to the library and show the children how to conduct a library search for a fiction book about a cat or cats. Each child could read their chosen story to a friend, a small group or the class, if they are confident.
- Talk with the children about cat's fur. Discuss the other types of coats that animals and creatures have. List them. Encourage the children to work in pairs to find two examples of animals or creatures with the following coats: hair, wool, feathers, scales, skin.
- Organise the children to work in pairs. One child describes their pet in detail, while the child who is listening draws the animal. They then swap places and repeat the exercise.
- Talk about the amusing antics of cats and kittens. Ask the children to write a short story about a funny episode (fiction or non-fiction) involving a cat.

My Nana's cat is called Ginger. Ginger sleeps in Nana's knitting bag.

- Make paper bag puppets with the children. Draw or paint cat features, e.g. ears, whiskers, nose, mouth, eyes, onto cardboard and cut them out. Staple or glue the features onto a paper bag. The children may like to use one of the fiction stories they have read to present a play to the rest of the class. High achieving children may like to write their own play.

Ideas for maths

- In groups, ask the children to find out how many people in the class have cats, dogs, birds, etc. as pets. Show the children how to graph the information and share it with the class.

Tally Sheet

Cats	Dogs	Birds
IIII	II	I

Bar Graph

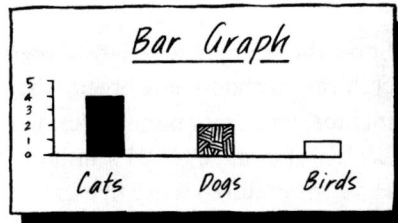

Books to share and compare
- *Big cat dreaming*, Margaret Wild, Penguin Books, 1996.
- *Charlie Anderson*, Barbara Abercrombie, Puffin Books, 1990.
- *Hairy Maclary Scattercat*, Lynley Dodd, Mallinson Rendel, 1988.

This activity develops the children's oral language skills by encouraging them to speak clearly and descriptively, and listen attentively.

Dogs

Creating the atmosphere

- Encourage the children to talk about pets they know.
- Discuss the differences between animals that are kept as pets and animals in the wild.

Focusing on the book

- Discuss the title and cover page photograph.
- Turn to the title page and talk about the list of contents and the corresponding page numbers.
- Read each chapter heading with the children. Ask them to turn to a chapter of their choice. Check that they are using the page numbers as reference.
- Return to the first chapter on p. 2. Read this with the children, discussing the photographs and/or illustrations.
- Read the linear question of the bottom of the page. Encourage the children to find the answer within the text of this double page. Turn to the next page and confirm the answer which is on the corresponding colour band at the bottom of the page.
- Discuss the reason for the alphabetical index on the inside back cover of the book. Demonstrate how to use the index, then observe and assist the children as they experiment with the new skill.

> As this is a non-fiction book, each chapter or paragraph can stand alone. Children do not have to hold the thread of a storyline in their minds.

Going beyond the book

- Read and sing *Bingo* (PM Readalongs: Down on the Farm).
- Read p. 13 of *Choosing a puppy* (PM Story Books Yellow Level). Have the children write and illustrate their own 'Puppy care' book.
- Talk about the ways dogs help us in the community. Make a list of other animals that people use. This activity could be completed as a whole class, in small groups, in pairs or individually. Some children may like to choose one 'helpful' animal to draw and write about.

> This activity requires the children to plan and make decisions.

Sheep give us wool.

We use wool to make warm clothes.

- Show the children a variety of books about different breeds of dogs. Ask the children to choose one breed. They can write a report about their chosen dog and include diagrams and pictures. Display the reports for others to read.
- Look at the range of PM Animal Facts books. Make some 'What am I?' cards. Have the children write five important clues about an animal on a card. They can draw a picture and write the name of the animal on the back of the card. The other children guess what the animal is and check on the back.

Blackline masters 5 and 6, pp.25–26.

- Show the children a number of advertisements (enlarged on the photocopier) from the 'Pets for sale' column of a newspaper. Talk about the features of the advertisements. Ask the children to write their own advertisements for one of the puppies featured on pp. 10–11 of *Dogs* (PM Animal Facts: Pets)

For Sale
Five black Labrador puppies
$100
Ph 289 0167

- Discuss and list the reasons why many people have dogs as pets.

Dogs help to protect us.
Dogs are good friends.
Dogs help blind people.
Dogs are fun to exercise with.

- Collect magazine pictures of dogs. Make a collage in the shape of a dog.
- Ask a dog trainer or vet to visit the classroom to talk to the children and perhaps conduct a demonstration. Involve the children in the arrangements by having them write letters or faxes, or plan a telephone conversation. Ensure that the children have questions prepared before the visit.
- List some of the types of dogs and their features, e.g. long hair, short legs, etc. Use this information to make accurate foil sculptures of different types of dogs. Crumple foil into dog shapes and secure them with pins or adhesive tape. Display with labels of each dog's breed.
- Challenge the children to find one interesting or unusual fact about dogs. Write each fact on a large piece of paper with a title.

Did you know?

Dogs put their tongues out when they want to cool down.

Books to share and compare

- *The most obedient dog in the world,*
  Anita Jeram,
  Walker Books, 1993.
- *Rosalie,*
  Joan Hewett,
  Lee & Shepard Books, 1987.
- *Hairy Maclary from Donaldson's Dairy,*
  Lynley Dodd,
  Mallinson Rendel, 1983.
- *Harry the dirty dog,*
  Gene Zion,
  The Bodley Head, 1960.

Presenting visual information is another important form of language communication.

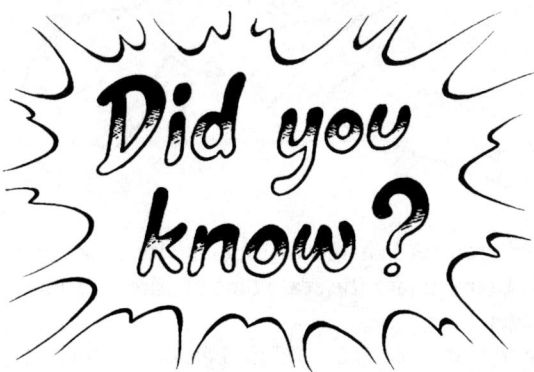

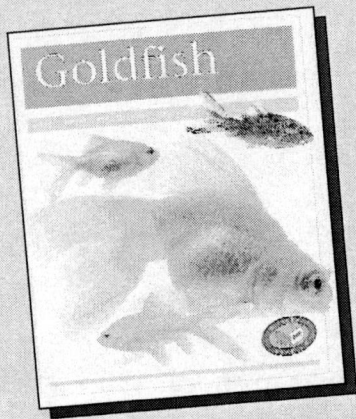

Goldfish

Creating the atmosphere

- Encourage the children to talk about pets they know.
- Discuss the differences between animals that are kept as pets and animals in the wild.

Focusing on the book

- Discuss the title and cover page photograph.
- Turn to the title page and talk about the list of contents and the corresponding page numbers.
- Read each chapter heading with the children. Ask them to turn to a chapter of their choice. Check that they are using the page numbers as reference.
- Return to the first chapter on p. 2. Read this with the children, discussing the photographs and/or illustrations.
- Read the linear question of the bottom of the page. Encourage the children to find the answer within the text of this double page. Turn to the next page and confirm the answer which is on the corresponding colour band at the bottom of the page.
- Discuss the reason for the alphabetical index on the inside back cover of the book. Demonstrate how to use the index, then observe and assist the children as they experiment with the new skill.

As this is a non-fiction book, each chapter or paragraph can stand alone. Children do not have to hold the thread of a storyline in their minds.

Going beyond the book

- Ask the children what they know about goldfish. Ask them what they would like to find out about goldfish. Before they read *Goldfish* (PM Animal Facts: Pets), make an enlarged book, recording the children's questions. Encourage them to find the answers to their questions while reading the book. Record the answers and illustrate the book.
- Divide the children into groups to compile lists of equipment needed to set up an aquarium for goldfish in the classroom. Discuss and compare the lists.
- Set up an aquarium in the classroom. Talk about the purpose of each piece of equipment.
- Have a goldfish naming competition. List the suggested names. The children could vote for the names they like. Select the most popular names.

Language experience books provide additional reading material.

Goldie   Flash   Zippity

- Read a variety of legends to the children. As a shared writing activity, make up a short legend about how fish came to live under the sea. Some children may like to paint pictures to go with the legend.
- In pairs, ask the children to pretend that there is a child in their class who has never seen goldfish before and knows nothing about them. The children need to describe a goldfish in detail. They can also make a list of the things necessary for the care of goldfish.

Blackline masters 7 and 8, pp.27–28.

- Read *The rainbow fish* (Marcus Pfister, North-South Books, 1992) to the children. The children could design their own 'rainbow fish'. Use a folded piece of thick paper and decorate it with bright coloured paints and tin foil. Cut out the fish and staple the edges leaving a hole. Fill with crumpled newspaper to create a 3-D effect. Make a large mural using crepe paper to represent water-weed and blue or green cellophane for water.

- Visit a pet shop or specialist goldfish shop. Before the visit, have the children prepare appropriate questions to ask. As an extension activity, some children may like to write a report of the visit.
- Let the children observe the goldfish in the class aquarium for a while. Encourage them to describe the goldfish and their environment to each other. Use these descriptions to motivate the children to write about goldfish. Some children may like to imagine they are goldfish and write from this perspective.
- Talk about fish that live in salt water and fish that live in fresh water. Make up a chart with this information.

Ideas for maths

- Look at p. 5 of *Goldfish* (PM Animal Facts: Pets). Use the measurement activity on this page to reinforce concepts of measurement. Measure the goldfish on the page. Ask the children to measure their feet. They could use the data to make a two page booklet.

Books to share and compare
- *The rainbow fish*, Marcus Pfister, North-South Books, 1992.
- *The fish who could wish*, John Bush, Oxford University Press, 1991.

Shared observations will help to develop the children's understanding and increase their curiosity.

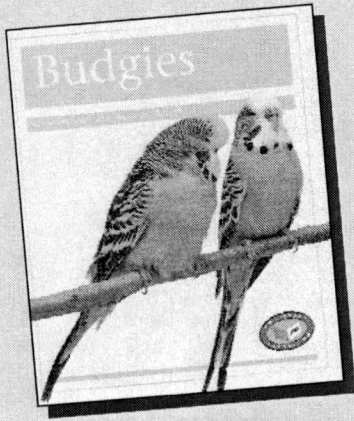

Budgies

Creating the atmosphere

- Encourage the children to talk about pets they know.
- Discuss the differences between animals that are kept as pets and animals in the wild.

Focusing on the book

- Discuss the title and cover page photograph.
- Turn to the title page and talk about the list of contents and the corresponding page numbers.
- Read each chapter heading with the children. Ask them to turn to a chapter of their choice. Check that they are using the page numbers as reference.
- Return to the first chapter on p. 2. Read this with the children, discussing the photographs and/or illustrations.
- Read the linear question of the bottom of the page. Encourage the children to find the answer within the text of this double page. Turn to the next page and confirm the answer which is on the corresponding colour band at the bottom of the page.
- Discuss the reason for the alphabetical index on the inside back cover of the book. Demonstrate how to use the index, then observe and assist the children as they experiment with the new skill.

> As this is a non-fiction book, each chapter or paragraph can stand alone. Children do not have to hold the thread of a storyline in their minds.

Going beyond the book

- Give the children a selection of poems about birds. Have the children paste the poems into small books. Show them how to number the pages and create a contents page. Have them illustrate the poems and share their books with the rest of the class.

> Ensure the children understand the purpose and use of a contents page.

- Show the children how to write an acrostic poem about budgies. Ask the children to write the word 'budgie' on a piece of paper. They then think of words to describe a budgie which begin with each letter of the word. Share the poems with the class.

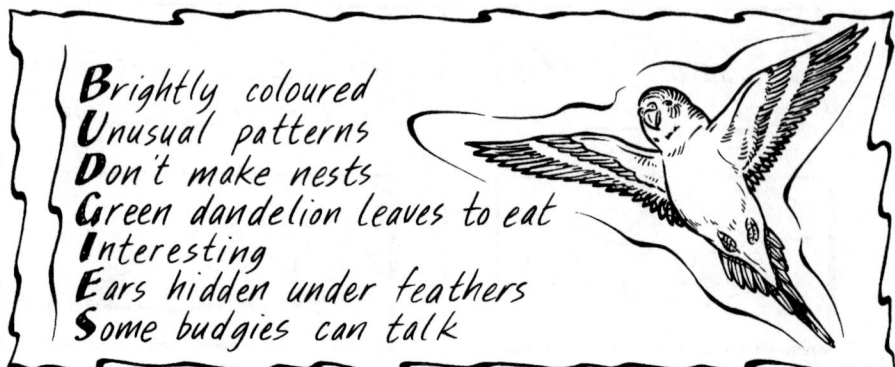

Brightly coloured
Unusual patterns
Don't make nests
Green dandelion leaves to eat
Interesting
Ears hidden under feathers
Some budgies can talk

Blackline masters 9 and 10, pp.29–30.

- Pose the following questions to the children:
    'Should birds be kept as pets?'
    'Are cages the best place to keep them?'
    'How would you change a bird cage to make it more enjoyable for a bird?'
  The children could discuss the questions in pairs, and report back to the class.
- Ask the children to pretend they are judging a class budgie competition. They could make a list of all the things they are looking for in a winning budgie.

Budgie Competition
The brightest colour.
The loudest cheep.

> Encourage the children to reason and justify their answers.

- Go bird watching in a park, the bush or at the beach. Have the children record the different birds that they see or hear. Share results.
- Prepare individual booklets with unfinished sentences about budgies for the children to complete. Use paper which is cut in the shape of a bird cage. Number the pages and include a contents page. Once completed, hang the books from an old umbrella frame or bicycle wheel.
- Give the children 'budgie shaped' paper. Ask them to write facts about budgies on it. Display by hanging the bird facts from an old branch with nylon.

> Motivate the children to show curiosity in the natural environment.

Books to share and compare
- *Tim's budgie*,
  Nigel Snell,
  Hodder & Stoughton, 1989.
- *Know your pet: Budgies*,
  Anna & Michael Sproule,
  Wayland Publications, 1988.

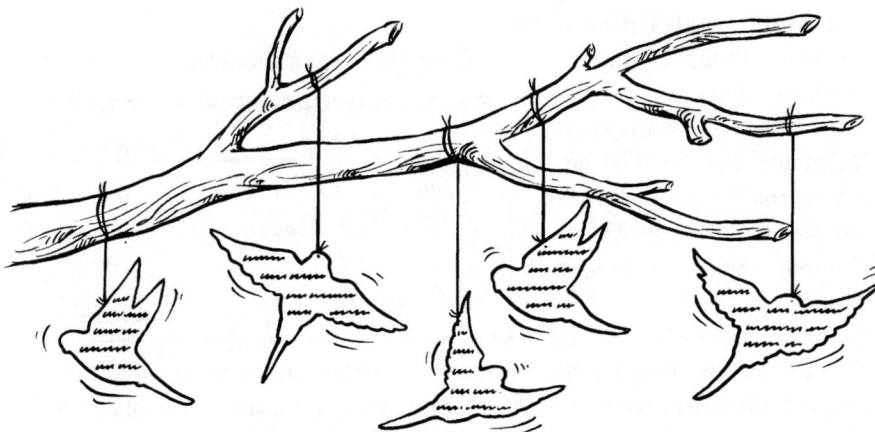

- Look at the budgies' beaks on p. 6 and p. 10 of *Budgies* (PM Animal Facts: Pets). Talk about the shape, size and use of beaks, e.g. opening seeds, eating, climbing etc. The children could research the beaks of other birds by looking at books in the class or school library. They could record the name of the bird (some children may like to sketch it), and the shape, size and use of the beak. Encourage the children to compare their findings with the information they have about budgies. Discuss all findings as a group.
- Talk with the children about budgies' eggs and the eggs of other birds. Discuss the fact that not only birds lay eggs. Challenge the children to discover other animals which also lay eggs, e.g. crocodiles, fish, lizards.
- Use the information in *Budgies* for the children to make oral presentations to the rest of the class.

Mice

Creating the atmosphere

- Encourage the children to talk about pets they know.
- Discuss the differences between animals that are kept as pets and animals in the wild.

Focusing on the book

- Discuss the title and cover page photograph.
- Turn to the title page and talk about the list of contents and the corresponding page numbers.
- Read each chapter heading with the children. Ask them to turn to a chapter of their choice. Check that they are using the page numbers as reference.
- Return to the first chapter on p. 2. Read this with the children, discussing the photographs and/or illustrations.
- Read the linear question of the bottom of the page. Encourage the children to find the answer within the text of this double page. Turn to the next page and confirm the answer which is on the corresponding colour band at the bottom of the page.
- Discuss the reason for the alphabetical index on the inside back cover of the book. Demonstrate how to use the index, then observe and assist the children as they experiment with the new skill.

> As this is a non-fiction book, each chapter or paragraph can stand alone. Children do not have to hold the thread of a storyline in their minds.

Going beyond the book

- Sing the song *Three blind mice* as a musical activity.
- Ask the children to design, draw and write about an interesting home for a pet mouse. They could work in pairs. Share the designs with the rest of the class. Discuss the features of each design.
- Keep a pet mouse in the classroom. Read *Mice* (PM Animal Facts: Pets) with the children. Help them make a chart showing how to care for the mouse. Let the children have turns feeding the mouse and cleaning its cage. The children may like to set up a class roster.

How to care for our mouse
- *Change the water every day.*
- *Feed the mouse birdseed, nuts and fruit.*
- *Clean the cage.*

- Read *The lion and the mouse* (PM Story Books Blue Level). The children could work individually or in pairs to think of other fictional situations where mice could be helpful. Share all the ideas with the class. Encourage the children to illustrate these ideas and compile them into an enlarged book.

A mouse could crawl into small places to find lost toys.

A mouse could clean up crumbs off the floor.

- Have a class debate on the topic 'Mice are better pets than dogs'. The speakers' ideas could be recorded on a large chart. Ensure that the audience know that their role is to listen carefully to the reasons presented by the speaker. A discussion could be conducted with the audience later.

Blackline masters 11 and 12, pp.31–32.

- Set up individual project books for each child to complete over a period of a few days. Number the pages and include a contents page. Some children could finish incomplete sentences such as 'Mice eat …' or 'Mice live …'. High achieving children should be encouraged to plan their projects themselves. Talk about the importance of including essential information.

Mice have two ears, two eyes, four paws, a nose, some teeth, some whiskers and a long tail.	Mice eat birdseed, nuts, bread, ham, cheese, dog biscuits, and apples.

- Provide opportunities for the children to display their knowledge about mice in a variety of ways:
  lists; recording facts on audio tape; project books; murals; or wall stories.
- Make a dictionary mobile of words about mice.
- Help a group of children to plan a series of photographs of the class mouse. Have the children photograph the mouse doing a variety of different things, e.g. eating, sleeping, playing, cleaning etc. Use the photographs for discussion or writing.

Mice
little
fast
sharp teeth
nibble food
little paws

- Talk about animals and insects that are pests. Discuss the reasons why these animals are not popular, e.g. disease, destruction of crops, smell etc. Encourage the children to research these animals at home or at the library and share their findings with the rest of the class.
- Have the children find words in the book which describe the actions of mice, e.g. sleep, run up and down, jump, play, run round and round. Write these actions on a chart. Go outside and ask the children to demonstrate the actions. Talk about other animals that move in a similar way.
- Ask the children to imagine what sort of food a mouse would store in its kitchen, if mice had kitchens. The children could then draw this. Encourage them to show clearly the different foods featured in the book.
- Play a game of 'Cat and mouse'. All but two children stand in a circle and hold hands. One child is the mouse and one is the cat. The object of the game is for the cat to chase and catch the mouse. The children standing in the circle help the cat or the mouse by lifting or lowering their linked arms to 'open' or 'close' the gates.
- In pairs, the children could make a miniature model of a mouse's cage. Cut a hole in the lid of a shoe box. Cover the hole with clear plastic. Build models of the equipment found in a mouse's cage. Make a 'spy hole' in the end of the box.
- Begin an 'Interesting animal facts' book which can be added to, during the year.

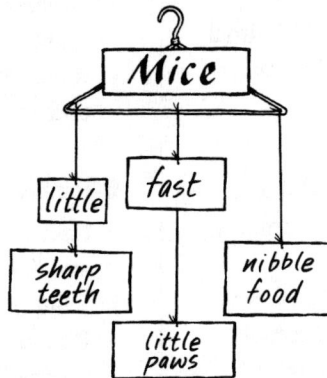

> Providing opportunities for the children to choose their own methods of publication increases their sense of ownership.

Books to share and compare
- **Whose mouse are you?**, Robert Krauss, Puffin Books, 1969.
- **Mice**, Ron Wilson, A & C Black, 1984.
- **House mouse**, Barrie Watts, A & C Black, 1991.

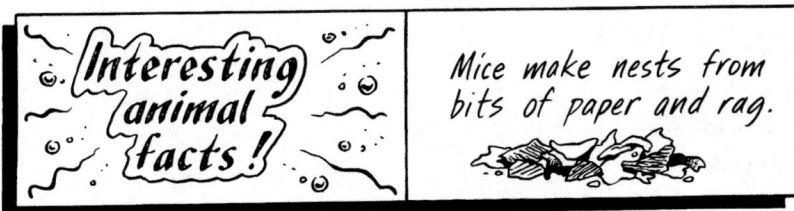

Interesting animal facts!	Mice make nests from bits of paper and rag.

Using the Blackline masters

Blackline master 1 *Guinea pigs*

- Demonstrate how to search the text to verify the information.
- Encourage the children to draw a detailed illustration related to the instructions.

Blackline master 2 *Guinea pigs*

- Discuss plurals within the meaningful context of the book.
- Demonstrate the use of plurals by writing some words on the whiteboard.
- Ask the children to draw three or more animals in the spaces provided.
- Show the children pp. 4–5 of *Guinea pigs* (PM Animal Facts: Pets) to help them answer the second section.

Blackline master 3 *Cats*

- Read pp. 12–15 of *Cats* (PM Animal Facts: Pets) with the children. Discuss the fact that the adult animal and its young often have different names.
- Ask the children to complete the sentences.
- Some children may need ideas to help them complete the second section of the Blackline master.

Blackline master 4 *Cats*

- Discuss the things that cats like to do.
- Ask the children to complete the sentences and draw detailed pictures. Encourage the children to draw on their own experiences with cats or kittens for ideas.

Blackline master 5 *Dogs*

- Discuss the meaning of the word 'fact' with the children.
- Have them find at least one fact in the book to discuss within the group situation.
- Encourage the children to do the writing and drawing independently.

Blackline master 6 *Dogs*

- Talk about the ways dogs help people.
- Ensure the children know how to write a list.
- Ask the children to complete the list and to choose one helpful activity to illustrate.

Blackline master 7 *Goldfish*

- Look at the diagram of the goldfish with the children.
- Use *Goldfish* (PM Animal Facts: Pets), pp. 4–5, to ensure the children can identify the various parts of the goldfish.

- Encourage the children to write a descriptive sentence about each word.

Blackline master 8 *Goldfish*

- Read and discuss the checklist with the children. Encourage them to tick the box as each activity is completed.
- Read the text in each box with the children.
- Ask the children to find the information in the book before they complete each sentence.

Blackline master 9 *Budgies*

- Discuss with the children what they know about budgies.
- Read through the blackline master with the children and ensure they understand the directions.

Blackline master 10 *Budgies*

- Revise opposites by writing words on the whiteboard and asking the children to guess their opposites.
- Read the instructions with the children.
- Encourage them to search the text of the book before proceeding with the Blackline master.

Blackline master 11 *Mice*

- Talk about the different foods that mice like to eat.
- Have several copies of non-fiction pet books for the children to read, e.g. *Goldfish*, *Cats*, *Dogs*, *Guinea pigs*, *Budgies* (PM Animal Facts: Pets).
- Ask the children to choose another pet, and write and draw about the food it eats.
- Have a discussion with the children about the food they eat.

Blackline master 12 *Mice*

- Revise compound words within the meaningful context of the story.
- Demonstrate how to complete a similar sentence to those in part 2.
- Encourage the children to listen to the sentence read aloud using alternative verb tenses. Ask them which one sounds the best.
- The children can complete the sentences and the illustration.

Name: _____ Date: _____

Read *Guinea pigs*.
Now read these sentences.
Write | Yes | or | No |

Some guinea pigs are black and white. ☐

Guinea pigs have long tails. ☐

Guinea pigs live in a cage. ☐

Guinea pigs like to eat clean hay and grain. ☐

Guinea pigs don't drink water. ☐

A newborn guinea pig has its eyes closed. ☐

Baby guinea pigs are not born with teeth. ☐

Baby guinea pigs like to play. ☐

Another name for a guinea pig is a cavy. ☐

Turn this page over.
Draw a picture of a guinea pig.
Write these words in the right places on its body.

| ears | eyes | nose | mouth | legs |

| paws | claws | teeth |

Name: _____ Date: _____

One guinea pig

Lots of guinea pigs

One cat

Lots of _____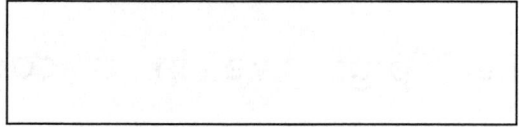

One dog

Lots of _____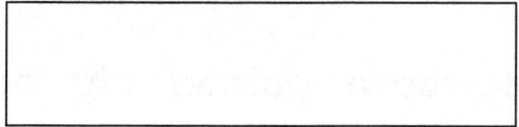

One mouse

Lots of _____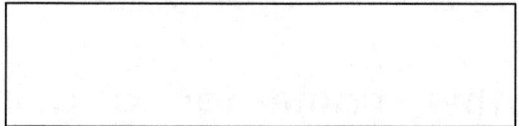

A guinea pig has

two _____, two _____,

four _____ and four _____.

But a guinea pig has no _____.

Name: _____ Date: _____

A baby cat is called a kitten.

A baby dog is called a _____.

A baby cow is called a _____.

A baby sheep is called a _____.

A baby horse is called a _____.

A baby goat is called a _____.

A baby pig is called a _____.

piglet

puppy

calf

lamb

kid

foal

Draw a picture of another animal and its baby.
Can you write the name of **this** baby animal?

Name: _____ Date: _____

Cats and kittens like to do lots of things.

play	catch	eat	lick
climb	drink	purr	smell

Put the best word in each space.

Cats _____ water and milk.

Cats _____ meat and fish and canned cat food.

Some cats _____ mice and rats.

Cats have claws to help them _____ trees.

Kittens like to _____ at catching things.

Kittens cannot see, but they can _____.

Mother cats _____ their kittens

to make them clean.

When cats are warm and happy, they _____.

Turn this page over and draw a picture
of a cat or a kitten playing or climbing
or catching something.

Name: _____ Date: _____

Read the book *Dogs* (PM Animal Facts: Pets) again.

Find two interesting facts about dogs.

Now draw and write about these interesting facts.

Book title: _____

Authors: _____

Facts: _____

Draw a picture to go with each fact.

Name: _____ Date: _____

Look at pages 14–16 of *Dogs* (PM Animal Facts: Pets).
Read about how dogs help people.

Can you think of other ways that dogs help people?

Write a list of ways dogs help people.

Dogs help us ...

_____

_____

_____

_____

_____

Draw a picture of a dog helping someone.

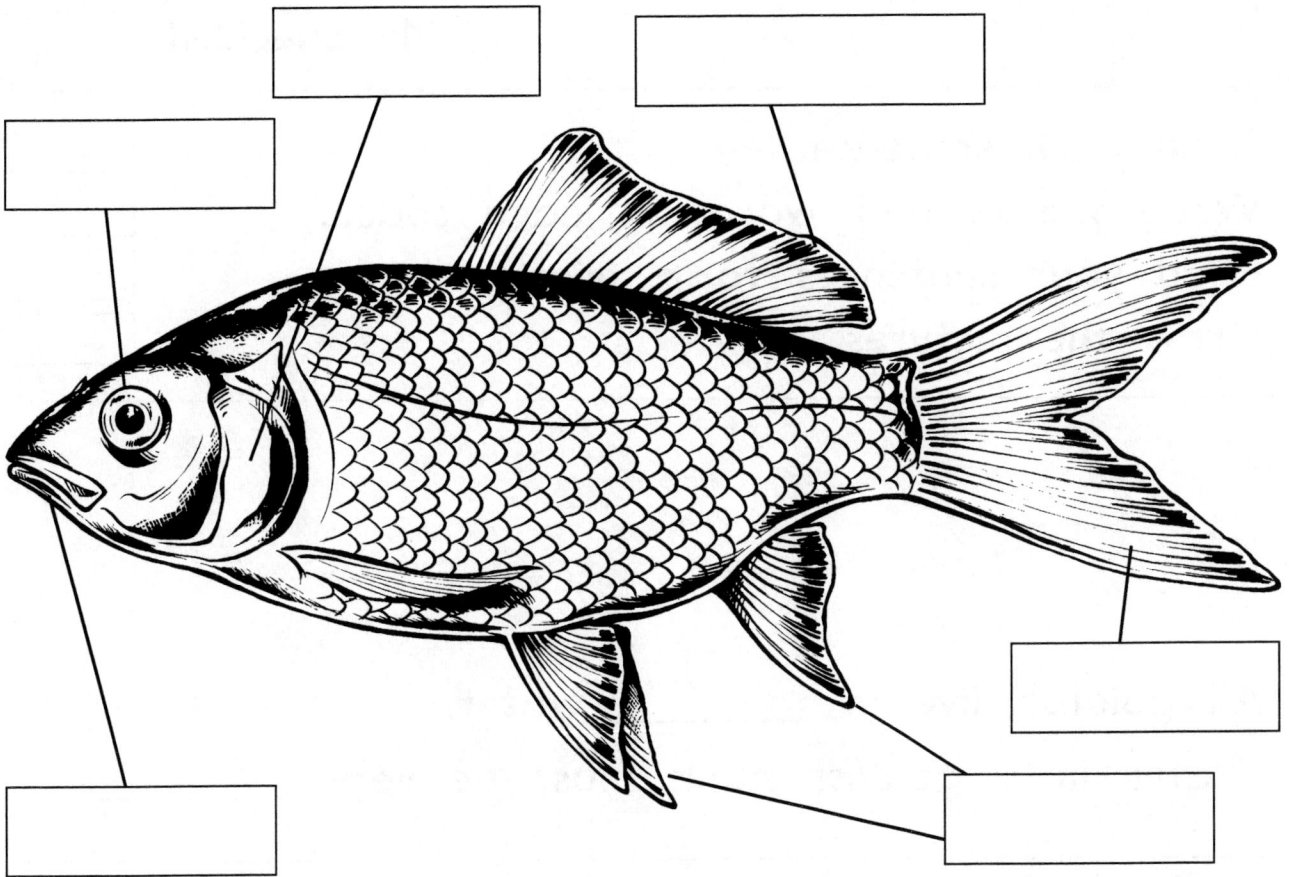

gills tail mouth back fin eye fins

Write a sentence about each of these words:
gills   fins   tail

Name: _____ Date: _____

My checklist ☑

Read each sentence.	☐
Write the correct words in each space.	☐
Read your sentences to a friend.	☐
Draw the pictures.	☐

All goldfish live in _____ water.

Water in a goldfish tank must be very _____.

Green water-weed puts _____ into the water in goldfish pools and tanks.

A goldfish has _____ to take air out of the water.

Water goes into its _____ and out of its gills.

Name: _____ Date: _____

Write two things that you know about budgies.

1. _____

2. _____

Write a list of the food that budgies like to eat.

_____

_____

_____

Draw a picture of a budgie. Colour your picture carefully.

Name: _____ Date: _____

These words are opposites:

inside   outside

These words are opposites, too: **wild   tame**

Some pet budgies can be very tame.

Write some facts and draw some pictures about **wild** budgies and **tame** budgies.

I know that wild budgies ...

_____

_____

_____

I know that tame budgies ...

_____

_____

_____

Turn this page over. Draw two pictures.

1. A wild budgie up in a tree.

2. A pet budgie inside a cage.

Name: _____ Date: _____

Draw some of the things that **mice** like to nibble.

Mice eat ...

Choose another pet.
Draw the food that it eats.

_____ eat ...

Draw the food that you eat.

I eat ...

Name: _____ Date: _____

1. Find two small words in each big word.

upstairs   _____   _____

downstairs   _____   _____

sometimes   _____   _____

inside   _____   _____

mousetraps   _____   _____

birdseed   _____   _____

2. Put the best word in each space.

Mice are little and are good at _____.

| hide |
| hiding |
| hid |

They _____ up and down their ladders.

| run |
| running |
| ran |

Sometimes they _____.

| jump |
| jumping |
| jumped |

They eat and _____ downstairs.

| play |
| playing |
| played |

Sometimes they _____ up and hold

things when they eat.

| sit |
| sitting |
| sat |

Turn this page over and draw a picture
of a mouse in a big cage.
Don't forget to draw something for it to play with.

PM Story Books Green Level

Set A
The *Naughty Ann*
Brave Triceratops
The clever penguins
Pete Little
House hunting
Candle-light

Set B
The flying fish
The rescue

Mrs Spider's beautiful web
Ben's tooth
Ten little garden snails
The fox who foxed
The little red bus

Snow on the hill
The babysitter
Father Bear's surprise

The island picnic
The flood
Pepper's adventure
The waving sheep
The cross-country race

After the flood
Joey
Try again, Hannah

PM Story Books Orange Level

Set A
The Dinosaur Chase
The Biggest Fish
Jack and Chug
Toby and BJ
Toby and the Big Tree
The Toy Farm

Set B
Sarah and the Barking Dog
Pterosaur's Long Flight
Just One Guinea Pig

Jessica in the Dark
Toby and the Big Red Van
Mitch to the Rescue

Set C
Rebecca and the Concert
Lost in the Forest
The Careful Crocodile
Roller Blades for Luke
The Busy Beavers
Two Little Goldfish

PM Traditional Tales and Plays Orange Level

Chicken-Licken
The Gingerbread Man

The Three Little Pigs
The Tale of the Turnip

The Little Red Hen
The Three Billy Goats Gruff

PM Animal Facts: Pets Orange Level

Guinea Pigs
Cats

Dogs
Mice

Budgies
Goldfish

PM Story Books Turquoise Level

Set A
When the Volcano Erupted
Monkey Tricks
The Cabin in the Hills
Jonathan Buys a Present
Nelson, the Baby Elephant
Toby and the Accident

Set B
Little Dinosaur Escapes
Rescuing Nelson
Number Plates

The Seat Belt Song
Bird's Eye View
The Hailstorm

Set C
Grandad's Mask
Ant City
The Nesting Place
Jordan's Lucky Day
Riding to Craggy Rock
The Race to Green End

PM Traditional Tales and Plays Turquoise Level

Goldilocks and the Three Bears
Stone Soup

Little Red Riding Hood
The Ugly Duckling

The Brave Little Tailor
The Elves and the Shoemaker

PM Animal Facts: Animals in the Wild Turquoise Level

Apes and Monkeys
Brown Bears

Elephants
Hippos

Kangaroos
Lions and Tigers